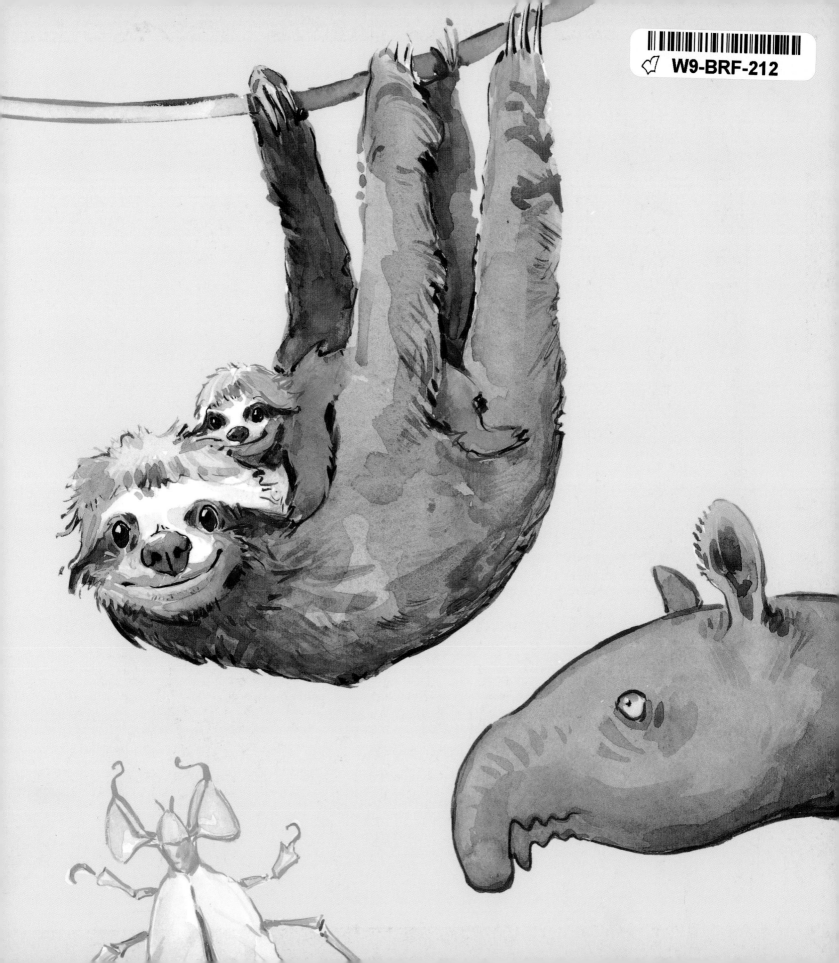

For Dave

First Edition
1 3 5 7 9 10 8 6 4 2
F850-6835-5-10288
This book is set in 15-point Footlight Light.
The artwork was done in watercolor.
Designed by Joann Hill
Printed in Singapore
Library of Congress Cataloging-in-Publication Data on file.
ISBN 978-1-4231-1389-8
Reinforced binding
Visit www.hyperionbooksforchildren.com

Strange Creatures

The Story of Walter Rothschild and His Museum

Lita Judge

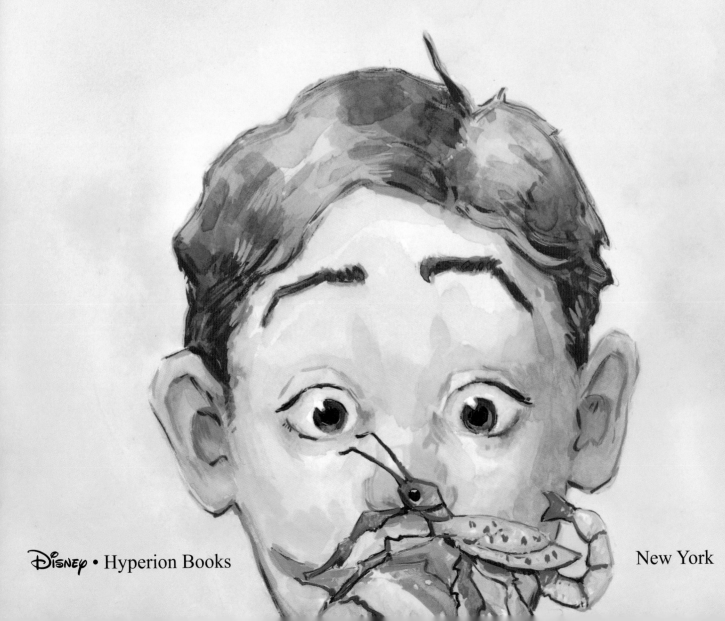

Disney • Hyperion Books

New York

Walter, the son of Lady Emma and Lord Nathan Rothschild, was a very unusual boy. He was born in 1868 and grew up on a great estate outside London. Here he had an entire world to explore, with a house as big as a palace and acres of gardens. There was a greenhouse for growing cacti, another for exotic orchids, and one just to grow flowers for the Queen's birthday. Walter's father was banker to the Queen of England. In fact, all of Walter's relatives were bankers. He was nearly the richest boy in the world, but that's not what made him unusual.

Walter was so shy he barely spoke. His parents feared that other children would tease him at school, so they kept him home, where he was tutored by a governess. But Walter spent all his time collecting bugs, birds, and animals. He didn't need words when he searched for butterflies in the garden. Walter had no friends, but he loved every creature that crawled, slithered, or flew.

One evening his father bellowed, "This is NOT what is expected of a Rothschild! You must learn to behave properly."

When Father yelled, Walter felt like a snail—small and curled up in a shell.

The next day he overheard his parents arguing.

"He's half-baked!" Father snapped.

"He's just lonely," Mother protested. "He'll grow out of it."

Father stomped back and forth. "He'll never be able to take over the family business. He won't amount to a penny."

SM VON ROTHSCHILD

Walter worried that his father was right.

His governess took him to Piccadilly to watch a circus parade. For the first time, Walter saw monkeys, zebras, and camels. He was so excited, his feet hopped, his knees wobbled, and words started swarming in his mind.

When he got home, he burst out, "Mother, Father, I'm going to collect animals from all over the world and build a museum, and I'm going to call it *My Museum!*" He didn't even stop to take a breath. This time, it was Father who had nothing to say.

Walter was only seven, but he began planning for his museum. He dreamed it would have animal specimens like a natural history museum, but also live animals. The family knew explorers who traveled the world to bring back animals for the London Zoo. Walter announced that he would like to use his allowance to buy a kangaroo.

"Perhaps it will help him get over his shyness," Mother pleaded. Father finally agreed.

Soon there were several kangaroos running free in the estate park. Walter cared for them with the help of a gamekeeper. His parents barely noticed when he added a wallaby or when he dashed by with a flock of kiwis trailing behind him. Walter loved the flightless little birds.

But his mother did mind when a giant lizard escaped and ate her prizewinning lilies.

"Walter!" she screamed.

When Walter turned twelve, the Natural History Museum opened a magnificent building in London. Walter imagined his own collection, now stored in garden sheds, displayed like this someday in a palace of wonders. He raced home and looked over his beetles, then gathered his courage to give some to Albert Günther, the head of the zoology department at the museum. Albert immediately became Walter's first true friend and mentor.

Walter lived in a time when many of the world's animals were unknown to science. Far-off jungles and uncharted islands were still waiting to be explored. He already had an encyclopedia of knowledge in his head about insects, birds, and animals that had been discovered, but he wanted to describe new species from unexplored lands. Albert knew that Walter was an unusual boy, not because of the way he struggled to speak, but because he was brilliant.

Walter's father didn't appreciate his son's brilliance. As Walter neared adulthood, Father demanded he stop spending all his time with bugs, and insisted he start work at the bank.

Walter reluctantly reported to his new life at the family firm. Achieving his own dreams seemed impossible.

But Walter's plans for his museum couldn't be dimmed. Now that he was working, he could afford to fund an expedition to discover animals in unexplored regions. He planned a great voyage and hired explorers to collect birds from newly charted islands in the South Pacific. Father wouldn't allow him to leave his job, but Walter traveled in his imagination through the southern seas each time he unpacked a crate the explorers sent back.

Walter studied the preserved birds carefully. He found tiny differences between specimens that most people would never notice, and began describing new species. Some of his finds from the expedition became the biggest news events in the scientific community.

Finally, Father agreed to a compromise. Walter would continue working at the bank, but his parents gave him land on the estate to construct a building large enough to house his entire collection.

Walter immediately funded more expeditions. Explorers shipped back birds and mammals, reptiles, fish, and insects from the far corners of the globe. Walter had animals no one had seen before. He began writing about his new discoveries, and invited scientists to study the animals that now lived on the estate, and his specimens. His collection would revolutionize the world's knowledge. The museum neared completion as he celebrated his twenty-fourth birthday.

At last the day arrived. Walter threw open the doors of his collection, showing the enormous variety of the world's beautiful and strange creatures.

Crowds of people lined up to see okapis from the Congo, capybaras from Colombia, and marabou storks. They gawked at giant cassowaries, spiny anteaters, and even fossils of prehistoric beasts.

Walter created the largest zoological collection ever gathered by one man, and was respected throughout the world for his contribution to science. With the help of two lifelong assistants, he wrote twelve hundred books and scientific papers, and named five thousand new species. Animals that now bear the name Rothschild include butterflies, fish, a millipede, a fly, a lizard, a porcupine, a wallaby, a bird of paradise, and even a giraffe.

Walter never did make a good banker. He remained shy his entire life and didn't marry, but he was happy surrounded by the giant tortoises, cassowaries, and other animals that lived on the estate.

Eventually he inherited the title of Lord Rothschild and was known for his generosity to all who visited his museum.

But his most generous act was opening his collection to future generations of scientists, who forever changed our understanding of the world's diversity of creatures.

Author's Note

LIONEL WALTER ROTHSCHILD (1868–1937) was famous for his contributions to zoology and his eccentric passion for animals. As Lord Rothschild, Walter liked to make a splash driving a zebra-drawn carriage down Piccadilly Lane—the same street where he watched the circus parade as a boy.

His father, Lord Nathan Rothschild, was the first Jewish peer in England, and banker to Queen Victoria. I don't know exactly what Walter and his father said to each other, but it's been documented that Lord Rothschild was disappointed and frustrated by his son's speech difficulties and shyness. As the eldest son, expected to take over the family banking firm, Walter couldn't have found life easy. Through his passion and courage, Walter stood up to his father and created his own legacy—the museum he started at the age of seven. People still enjoy visiting Walter's museum, the Natural History Museum at Tring in Hertfordshire, United Kingdom.

I was immediately captivated by Walter Rothschild, partly because as a child I, too, grew up in a home filled with wild creatures. My grandparents were ornithologists, and they shared their home with birds of prey. Every summer I jumped at the chance to care for barn owlets and kestrel chicks, or to help nurse an injured eagle back to health. My grandparents benefited from the scientists who came before them. One of their greatest scientific mentors, Ernst Mayr, began his career with an expedition to Papua New Guinea, collecting specimens for Walter Rothschild. Later he was curator of Rothschild's collection of birds, now housed in New York's American Museum of Natural History.

Walter lived in a very different time, when travel to remote places was extremely difficult, and there were no movies and few detailed photographs of animals. In many cases, collecting animal specimens was the only way for scientists to study them closely and to differentiate between species.

The study of wildlife has changed over the years. It's no longer considered ethical to take animal specimens. Now we study living animals with binoculars, and record their behavior with cameras. Scientists catch wild birds and place numbered bands on their legs, then release them back into the wild without harming them. Though methods and attitudes are different today, scientists and museum visitors still learn from the collections gathered more than a hundred years ago by Walter Rothschild and others.

ACKNOWLEDGMENTS

I'd like to thank Alice Dowswell, Head of Interpretation and Education, and Paul Kitching, Museum Manager, at the National History Museum at Tring.

REFERENCES

Gray, Victor. "Something in the Genes: Walter Rothschild, Zoological Collector Extraordinaire." Transcript from a lecture delivered at The Royal College of Surgeons, London, 25 October 2007.

Rothschild, Miriam. *Walter Rothschild: The Man, the Museum and the Menagerie.* London: Natural History Museum, 2008.

WEB SITES

Natural History Museum at Tring: www.nmh.ac.uk/tring
Natural History Museum, London: www.nmh.ac.uk
American Museum of Natural History, New York: www.amnh.org